Ferrari

Rebecca Hawley

PowerKiDS press

New York

Published in 2007 by The Rosen Publishing Group, Inc.
29 East 21st Street, New York, NY 10010

First Edition

Editor: Joanne Randolph
Book Design: Ginny Chu
Book Layout: Kate Laczynski
Photo Researcher: Sam Cha

Photo Credits: All Photos © Getty Images.

Library of Congress Cataloging-in-Publication Data

Hawley, Rebecca.
  Ferrari / Rebecca Hawley. — 1st ed.
      p. cm. — (Superfast cars)
  Includes index.
  ISBN-13: 978-1-4042-3640-0 (library binding)
  ISBN-10: 1-4042-3640-6 (library binding)
  1. Ferrari automobile—History—Juvenile literature. I. Title.
  TL215.F47 H38 2007
  629.222'2—dc22
                                                    2006020268

Manufactured in the United States of America

Contents

The gray car is the Ferrari Superamerica and the red one is the F430. Both of these are superfast cars made by Ferrari.

What Is a Fast Car?

There are cars, and then there are fast cars. Fast cars are built to move quickly. They cut through the air and hold tightly onto the road. Their **engines** are powerful and **efficient**. The cars are also made to handle well. The driver can push the car to the edge and stay in control. That is a pretty powerful feeling. This is what makes so many people like fast cars.

The Ferrari symbol is a black horse on a yellow background. Yellow is the color of Ferrari's birth city, Modena, Italy.

The Prancing Horse

One of the best-known makers of fast cars is Ferrari. Enzo Ferrari started the Italian company in the mid-1940s. He used a **prancing** horse as the company's **symbol**.

Ferrari began using the horse on his cars when he met Countess Paolina in 1923. Her brother painted a prancing horse on his planes. The countess thought it would bring her brother good luck if Ferrari used the horse on his race cars.

Ferrari makes about 3,500 cars a year in its factory. The workers and many machines work together to build the cars, paint them, and get them ready for the road.

On the Cutting Edge

Ferrari spends a lot of time coming up with new **designs** for its cars. It wants to be on the cutting edge. It has **engineers** working to make a car that will cut through the air. It also wants the car to look cool. Some people spend their time on the engine of the car. They try to find new and better ways to build the engine. They want it to reach high **speeds** quickly.

Ferrari has its own testing center in Italy. Here is the Formula 1 test track, where the company makes sure its race cars are up to speed.

Entrata
Entrance

Putting It to the Test

Ferrari works hard to build the fastest and coolest cars. It wants to be sure these cars live up to the Ferrari name. Before it puts a new **model** on the road, the company tests the model. It wants to see how the car drives. It wants to see how the car handles **extreme** weather or bad roads. It also wants to find out how fast the car can go and how long it takes the car to reach its top speed.

The Enzo can reach 60 miles per hour (97 km/h) in just over 3 seconds. The car has special brakes, which allow it to stop quickly and safely.

Meet the Enzo

There are certain cars that really show what Ferrari stands for. The Enzo is one of them. This car was based on Ferrari's **Formula 1** race cars. When the car came out, in 2002, it was the world's fastest car made for use on the road! The Enzo can reach speeds of 217 miles per hour (349 km/h). There are no roads in the United States where you can even drive that fast! Ferrari only built 400 Enzos.

The F430 can hit 60 miles per hour (97 km/h) in just 4 seconds.

Meet the F430

In 2004, Ferrari presented the F430 to the world. This car is both beautiful and fast. The car can reach top speeds of 195 miles per hour (314 km/h). The car sticks to the road and handles corners well. This is important when you are moving so quickly!

Ferrari spent over 2,000 hours testing the car in a wind tunnel. It wanted to be sure that air would not slow the car down.

The price for the FXX was huge. In fact, it was the most costly new car ever sold.

Meet the FXX

It is hard to make great designs even better. Ferrari did it, though. In 2005, the FXX was built. Only 29 of these cars were made. This car is made to fit the body of its owner exactly. The engine has a special computer that helps the driver handle the car better. It also supplies Ferrari with facts about the car and how it is driving. This will help Ferrari make better cars.

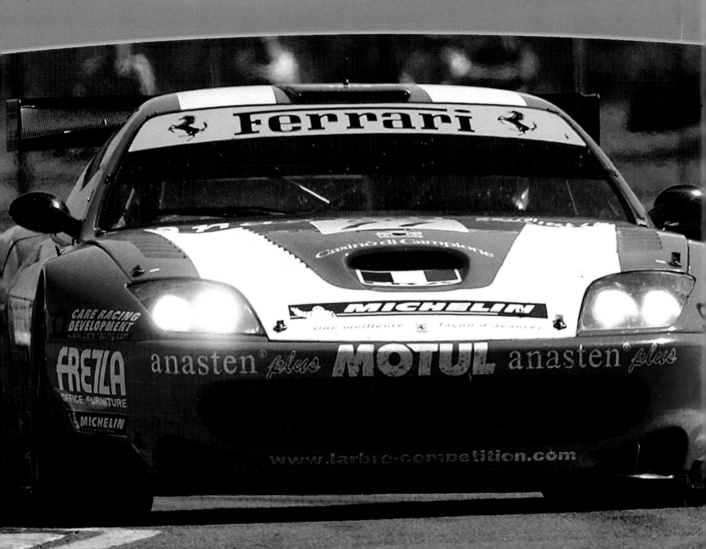

The Ferrari 550 Maranello speeds around the track during a race in England. Ferrari wins a lot of races.

At the Heart of Ferrari

Racing is at the heart of the Ferrari company. In fact, Enzo Ferrari's first love was racing. He would have been happy to have Ferrari make only race cars. However, making cars for everyday use is what keeps the company in business.

The company has its own racing team, called Scuderia Ferrari. The team has won many races over time. Ferrari is known as one of the best racing teams in the world.

Michael Schumacher, one of Ferrari's best drivers, competes in a Formula 1 race in Monaco. Schumacher often helps Ferrari's engineers design new cars.

Formula 1 and More

Ferrari works hard to design race cars that will **perform** well. Each year it tries to make better and faster cars. It wants these cars to handle better than any other cars on the track. It wants them to be faster than the other cars, too. Ferrari is best known for its Formula 1 race cars. It also makes many other kinds of race cars that race in **competitions** around the world. It is not easy to catch the prancing horse!

What Lies Ahead?

Ferrari is known for making cutting-edge cars. The company wants to live up to this as it comes up with new ideas for cars. Ferrari and other car companies make special cars called **concept** cars. These cars may never be built for everyday use. They push the idea of what cars can be to new places. No one knows what Ferrari's next superfast car will be like. We do know that we look forward to seeing it!

Glossary

competitions (kom-pih-TIH-shunz) Games or tests.

concept (KON-sept) An idea.

designs (dih-ZYNZ) The plans or the forms of something.

efficient (ih-FIH-shent) Done the quickest, best way possible.

engines (EN-jinz) Machines inside cars or airplanes that make the cars or airplanes move.

engineers (en-juh-NEERZ) Masters at planning and building engines, machines, roads, and bridges.

extreme (ik-STREEM) Going past the expected or common.

Formula I (FOR-myuh-luh WUN) A kind of car used in racing. It has one seat and its wheels are on the outside of the car's body.

model (MAH-dul) A kind of car.

perform (per-FORM) To carry out, to do.

prancing (PRANS-ing) A way of walking by pushing from the back legs and only lightly touching the front legs to ground.

speeds (SPEEDZ) How quickly something moves.

symbol (SIM-bul) Something, such as a picture, that stands for something else.

Index

Web Sites

Due to the changing nature of Internet links, PowerKids Press has developed an online list of Web sites related to the subject of this book. This site is updated regularly. Please use this link to access the list:
www.powerkidslinks.com/sfc/ferrari/